FLAT STANLEY

The Japanese Ninja Surprise

MASTER ODA NOBU
JAPAN

Read all of Flat Stanley's adventures

FLAT STANLEY

The Japanese Ninja Surprise

Created by Jeff Brown

Written by Sara Pennypacker

Illustrated by Jon Mitchell

EGMONT

EGMONT

We bring stories to life

The Japanese Ninja Surprise
First published in Great Britain 2011
by Egmont UK Limited
239 Kensington High Street
London W8 6SA
Text copyright 2009 by the Trust u/w/o Richard C. Brown
a/k/a Jeff Brown f/b/o Duncan Brown
Illustrations copyright 2009 by the Trust u/w/o Richard C. Brown
a/k/a Jeff Brown f/b/o Duncan Brown

ISBN 978 1 4052 5210 2

1 3 5 7 9 10 8 6 4 2

A CIP catalogue record for this title is available from the British Library

Printed and bound in Great Britain by the CPI Group

CONTENTS

Chapter One

The Seventeenth Samurai

'I salute you, Master Oda Nobu, greatest of all Samurai warriors!'

Arthur Lambchop bowed deeply from the waist as he spoke these words to the large poster hanging in the bedroom he shared with his brother, Stanley. The poster was for a movie called *The Seventeenth Samurai*. It showed two warriors – a tall samurai and a small ninja – looking very fierce. The tall samurai wore a long kimono and held a shining silver sword above his head. The small ninja was dressed exactly like Arthur, in black pyjamas with a strip of white cloth knotted at his waist and another tied around his forehead. He held his hands high, like the blades of knives ready to strike. Both warriors looked as if they could leap right out of the poster.

And then the small ninja did just that! 'Hiii-*yaaaah*!' he shouted, as he flew off the wall. He bounced high on the bed and landed with a *thud* in front of Arthur!

'Prepare to be defeated, Arthur-san!' the small ninja cried.

'Never!' Arthur leaped up, bounced high on the other bed, and landed with a *boom* on the opposite side of the room. 'It is you who will be defeated, Stanley-san!'

The small ninja was Arthur's older brother, Stanley Lambchop. Not long before, he had awoken to find that a large bulletin board had fallen upon him in the night, leaving him unharmed, but as flat as a pancake. By now, Stanley's family was used to his unusual shape, although Stanley wasn't always so happy about it.

At the moment, however, he was

enjoying himself tremendously. He and his brother chased each other around their bedroom, leaping on and off their beds with *thuds* and *booms* as they imitated the karate chops and kicks of their all-time favourite movie star, Oda Nobu.

'Boys!' Mrs Lambchop called. 'My teacups are rattling!'

'Is there nothing you fellows can do that doesn't make a ruckus?' called Mr Lambchop. 'How about a little quiet time?'

'Quiet time,' Stanley grumbled. He pulled off the white cloth around his head. 'Where's the fun in that?'

But then he had an idea. 'Arthur, let's write a letter to Oda Nobu! Maybe he'll write back and send us an autographed picture!'

'Or a ninja throwing star!' Arthur agreed, his grumpiness disappearing. He rummaged through his desk until he found a pad of paper and a ballpoint pen. 'You're good with words, Stanley. What should we say?'

'Hmmm,' Stanley said. 'How about "Dear Master Oda Nobu, we are your biggest fans ever. We have seen every one of your movies . . ."' He sent Arthur a questioning look.

Arthur shrugged. 'A hundred times?' he suggested.

Stanley smiled. 'Yes, that's good. Write "We have seen all of your movies at least a hundred times."'

Arthur began to write. Then he stopped. 'Stanley,' he said, 'Oda Nobu might think we're exaggerating.'

Stanley looked up at the poster, now with only one warrior on it, and bowed. 'You're right,' he said to Arthur. 'Honesty is an important part of the ninja code of honour. How about this: "We have seen every one of your movies several times."'

Arthur nodded and Stanley continued to dictate: '"Master Oda Nobu, it is too bad Japan is so far away. If you were closer, we would offer our services as your personal ninjas."'

Stanley paused. 'Wait a minute, Arthur!'

'"Wait . . . a . . . minute . . . Arthur,"' Arthur repeated, as he wrote the words down.

'No, don't write that!' Stanley said, and took the pad out of Arthur's hands. 'I have a better idea!' He dropped the pad on the desk and began to rummage around through the drawers.

'Aha!' he said, and held up a large brown envelope.

'There!' he said, and held up a sheet of postage stamps.

'Got it!' he said, and held up a thick black marker.

'Stanley, what's your idea?' Arthur asked.

Stanley placed many, many stamps in the corner of the big envelope. He uncapped the marker, printed something on the envelope in big block letters, and then held it up to show Arthur:

MASTER ODA NOBU
JAPAN

Stanley turned and bowed deeply to his brother. 'I salute you, Arthur-san. Now fold me up!'

Chapter Two

Fan Mail

Stanley Lambchop was no stranger to travelling in an envelope. Since becoming flat, he had been airmailed to visit a friend in California.

But Japan wasn't California. Japan was very, very far away.

Arthur had packed a good supply of rolled-up fruit snacks of course – so Stanley didn't go hungry. But the trip was long and boring, and folded up as he was, he was almost always uncomfortable. Finally, he felt the airplane bump to a landing – and the next voices he heard were Japanese! After many more long, uncomfortable hours of travel, being flipped and rolled, sorted and stacked, Stanley felt himself come to a rest.

In his eagerness to be released, Stanley began to stretch. He rocked from side to side and bounced up and down. That didn't get him out of the envelope, but it did get him some attention: Stanley heard footsteps, and then voices, coming closer. He could tell by the tone of the voices that the people were at first surprised by, and then suspicious of, the jumping envelope.

He was about to call out when someone shouted – and suddenly, the envelope was jerked up from where it lay.

With a sharp *rip*, light poured in from above his head. Without even thinking, Stanley flexed his cramped muscles and sprang from the envelope. He had only a moment to adjust his eyes to the scene before him when he was surrounded by . . . *ninjas!*

'Uh-oh,' Stanley thought, realising he was still dressed in his own ninja uniform. 'This isn't good!' But before he could say a word – or even think what he would

say – the ninjas attacked!

One flew through the air, his heel aimed straight at Stanley's head. Stanley quickly turned sideways, and because he was only half an inch thick, the ninja flew right past him and crashed into a wall! Another ninja threw a swift karate chop at Stanley, but Stanley folded himself in two, right at his waist, and the ninja's powerful hand sliced through empty air.

Now *all* the ninjas were on the attack! Stanley leaped and hovered and bent himself this way and that – and somehow managed to avoid every blow. Then something whistled by his ear, and Stanley heard a loud *thunk*! A shiny ninja throwing star was embedded in the wall.

He looked back to see who had thrown it at him and saw . . .

Oda Nobu!

'Wait!' Stanley shouted. 'Oda Nobu! I am not a ninja! I am just a fan! I've seen every one of your movies . . . several times!'

But the ninjas kept coming. Stanley bobbed and weaved and rolled and folded. 'It's only me!' he tried again. 'Stanley Lambchop, from America!'

Oda Nobu shouted a sharp command in Japanese, and the ninjas immediately stopped their attack. He stepped forward, his eyes very wide. 'You . . . are the . . . *Flat Stanley*?' he gasped.

Stanley nodded.

Oda Nobu turned to the ninjas.

He spoke sternly to them, the words rushing out like karate chops. Stanley understood only the last two: *'Flat Stanley!'*

The ninjas turned together to look at Stanley. They wore the same expression of awe as Oda Nobu, wide-eyed, their mouths hanging open. And then all at

once, they were laughing and bowing and shaking his hand.

'But,' Stanley said to Oda Nobu, 'how do you know who I am?'

Oda Nobu put his arm around Stanley's shoulder. 'Everyone in the whole world knows of Flat Stanley!'

The Ninja Way

Stanley was shown to a beautiful room in Oda Nobu's beautiful home. The walls, and even the doors, were made of delicate rice paper stretched across wooden frames. The only piece of furniture was a bed – a mat on a low platform, nearly on the floor.

A handsome kimono, embroidered with scarlet dragons, lay across the bed. Stanley slipped his arms into the sleeves and wrapped the kimono around himself. And around and around – apparently, kimonos were not styled for people with his shape – until finally he could tie the sash.

Then, one of the ninjas, the one who had thrown a flying kick at Stanley, appeared at the door. He gestured for Stanley to follow him.

At the end of a long sunlit hallway, the ninja slid open a rice paper door. There was Oda Nobu, seated on a straw mat in front of a low table. The movie star smiled as the ninja showed Stanley how to sit at the table, with his legs folded beneath him. For once, Stanley was grateful to be flat.

Oda Nobu gestured to the objects laid upon the table: ceramic bowls, a small scoop, a ladle and a covered jar. Beside these, water boiled in an iron pot above a flame.

'This is the tea ceremony, Stanley-san,' he said. 'It is a very ancient and very important tradition for Japanese people.'

Stanley watched as Oda Nobu measured powdered leaves into one of the ceramic bowls. Next, he ladled hot water into the bowl. He used the whisk to stir the tea. Stanley could tell that the careful motions had taken a lot of practice to learn.

The movie star bowed to Stanley and held the bowl out to him. Stanley bowed and took the bowl. Oda Nobu made a drinking gesture, and Stanley took a sip.

Stanley had never had tea before. It tasted . . .

Stanley searched for a word. Mrs Lambchop always said, 'If you can't say something nice, don't say anything at all.' Thinking about his mother reminded Stanley of the delicious hot chocolate she often made for special occasions. For an instant, homesickness washed over him, but he fought it, because *this* was a special occasion! And he wanted to tell Oda Nobu how much he appreciated the tea ceremony, even if the tea tasted . . .

And then a solution came to him: the tea tasted *interesting*!

He started to say this, but his host held a finger to his lips. 'We will talk soon,' he said, and reached for the bowl of tea. Stanley passed it to him, and Oda Nobu drank.

When they were finished, Oda Nobu cleaned all the tea ceremony's objects and arranged them neatly on the table. He and Stanley bowed to each other once again.

Then Oda Nobu stood and motioned for Stanley to follow him out of the tearoom and into a garden. They sat on a bench next to a fountain. Around the fountain were the smallest trees Stanley had ever seen.

'Bonsai,' Oda Nobu explained, as if he had read Stanley's mind. 'The art of training plants into pleasing miniature shapes. Another important tradition to my people. Yet another one is . . .' Oda Nobu looked directly at Stanley. 'Stanley-san,' he said, 'do you know the history of the ninja?'

'Sure,' Stanley said. 'Well, that is, I've seen all of your movies several times!'

Oda Nobu laughed. 'Ah, yes, of course!

But permit me to tell you a little more.' He picked up a stick, and in the sand he drew what looked like a charging seahorse. 'In the old times,' he said, 'Japan had many rulers. Each had his own kingdom, his own army, his own people and lands to protect.'

Oda Nobu drew small circles inside the larger outline, which Stanley now realised was the shape of Japan.

'Often these rulers would fight one another,' Oda Nobu continued. 'Like people everywhere, I am sorry to say. If you have something I want, and I believe I am more powerful than you, I just might decide to take it from you.'

Oda Nobu drew a line between two

circles in the sand. 'Of course, a ruler could use his army to take what he wanted,' he said. 'But often he believed it was better to use *ninjutsu*. Do you know what that word means, Stanley-san?'

'Well,' Stanley said, 'it sounds a little like *ninja*.'

'Yes, it does,' Oda Nobu said. '*Ninjutsu* means "the art of stealth". Ninjas are trained in the art of going undetected, of not being seen.'

'But,' Stanley said, 'I could see your ninjas pretty clearly.'

'Stanley-san, you are a very funny young man,' Oda Nobu said. 'And very honest in your observations. No, those men are not ninjas. They are my bodyguards. They just like to wear the ninja uniforms.'

'Bodyguards?' Stanley asked. 'Why would you need bodyguards? You're Oda Nobu!'

Oda Nobu shrugged. He looked embarrassed. 'Of course I don't need bodyguards. It is the movie studio. They think it makes their biggest movie star look even more important.'

Oda Nobu brushed away his drawings. He stood up and then bowed to Stanley. 'Stanley-san,' he said in a low voice, 'I must ask you a very important question. Will you be my personal ninja?'

Stanley couldn't believe his ears. His favourite movie star was asking him to be his personal ninja? Wait until Arthur heard about this!

'But,' Stanley said, 'why me? I don't know anything about karate or judo or jujitsu or any of that!'

'Remember *ninjutsu*, Stanley-san,' Oda Nobu said. 'The art of stealth. Your flatness allows you to go places and do things without being seen. It makes you the perfect ninja.'

Stanley couldn't believe his luck. Of course he would be Oda Nobu's personal ninja. *Of course* he would!

Flat Ninja!

Stanley was taken to Oda Nobu's personal
tailor, where he was measured for a ninja
uniform. It took the tailor a little time to
figure out how to fit a boy only half an
inch thick. But in the end the uniform
made of glossy black silk fitted him
perfectly. Stanley had never felt anything
quite so soft.

That night, Oda Nobu and Stanley rode through the crowded streets of Tokyo in the movie star's stretch limousine. The bodyguards followed in two other cars. They ate at one of Japan's most famous restaurants, where everyone, from the waiters to the other customers, smiled adoringly at Oda Nobu *and* Stanley. Even the chef bowed deeply when he delivered a long lacquered board covered with sushi to Oda Nobu's personal ninja.

If someone had told Stanley just a week before that he would be eating raw fish, and enjoying it, halfway around the world, he would have laughed. He was laughing now, but for a different reason. The food was delicious, even the seaweed and the smoked eel, and here he was sitting with his all-time favourite movie star!

After dinner, Oda Nobu took Stanley to a karaoke bar. They took turns singing one silly song after another. The crowd burst into wild applause after every one. Stanley drank three sodas that tasted exactly like bubble gum. He *loved* Japan!

Only one thing bothered him. Just why did Oda Nobu want a personal ninja anyway?

He found out the next day.

Oda Nobu took Stanley to an exhibition of famous kites at a big modern art museum. After admiring the amazing kites – some like ferocious dragons, others like nearly life-sized houses – Oda Nobu stopped to speak to a group of reporters. They spoke in Japanese, and Stanley didn't understand a word.

But then one of the reporters asked a question and pointed at Stanley, and everyone laughed. Oda Nobu looked at Stanley and shrugged. Then he picked Stanley up and smiled – and tossed him high into the air.

For a moment, Stanley hung there beside the kites on display, caught by the draft of the museum's air conditioning. It reminded him of other times he had flown like this – once in the park, with Arthur skilfully flying him with the other kites. Another time, he had been

caught by a gust of wind and flown out
dangerously close to a mountain. But
Arthur had cleverly thrown him a lasso
and guided him back to earth. Stanley
had always felt safe with his brother on
the ground below him.

Below him now, the crowd laughed and applauded. But then the air conditioners' breeze stopped and Stanley plummeted to the hard marble floor of the museum.

Everyone laughed, including Oda Nobu, who looked very proud of himself.

Everyone except Stanley.

Later that day, Oda Nobu took Stanley to the studio where he was making his latest movie. Stanley was thrilled to watch as his hero stood before the movie cameras and pretended to be the most famous samurai of all time.

But something was wrong. Time after time, Oda Nobu stopped the action to complain to a man Stanley guessed was the director. The actor would cover his face, squinting and frowning. The director would shrug, shake his head and start the scene over again.

The fourth time this happened, Oda Nobu seemed angry. He made the same gestures again. The director shook his head again. Then Oda Nobu pointed to Stanley and said something to the director. The director nodded.

The next thing Stanley knew, he found himself at the top of a long pole. He was stretched out on a frame, his hands and feet held by clips. A man on the ground held the pole, keeping Stanley between the bright sun and Oda Nobu's face below. With the sun no longer blazing on Oda Nobu's face, he was able to finish the scene.

And everyone was happy.

Everyone except Stanley.

That night, Oda Nobu held a big party at his home. 'It is in your honour, Stanley-san,' Oda Nobu said. 'The most famous people in Japan are coming to meet the most famous Stanley Lambchop.'

Stanley was pleased. Although he had grown tired of all the attention that had come with being a flattened boy, tonight he thought would be different.

The party was in his honour.

But then, in the middle of the party, some ladies pointed at Stanley and asked Oda Nobu a question. The ladies giggled. Oda Nobu shrugged as if to say, 'Why not?' He picked Stanley up off the floor and then expertly folded him into an origami star!

'Hey!' Stanley shouted, into the back of his own knee. 'Cut it out! Unfold me!'

Oda Nobu held the Stanley-star high above his head, so that everyone at the party could see it. Then, with one loud snap of his fingers, the star unfurled! And there was Stanley again, crumpled, creased and very unhappy.

So this was what having a 'personal ninja' meant to Oda Nobu! Having the world's only flat boy to show off to his adoring fans!

Stanley picked himself up off the floor. 'I am supposed to be a ninja,' he said to Oda Nobu. 'I am not a party trick!' And he marched off to his bedroom as straight as his creases would allow. He fell asleep trying not to think about how much he wished he were back at home with his family.

The next morning, Oda Nobu knocked softly at the door and then slid it open. He bowed low to Stanley, who was still in bed.

'Stanley-san,' Oda Nobu said. 'I am here to apologise most sincerely for my disrespectful behaviour yesterday. I wish to invite you to take a trip with me today. It is my way of asking for your forgiveness.'

Stanley studied Oda Nobu's face. The actor was not acting now.

'All right then,' Stanley said. 'When do we leave?'

Chapter Five

Off Like a Speeding Bullet!

An hour later, Stanley and Oda Nobu stood on the platform of the *Shinkansen* – Japan's famous bullet train! Oda Nobu held on to Stanley's hand tightly. Even so, as the big sleek train whooshed into the station, Stanley felt himself lifted ever-so-slightly off his feet. Oda squeezed his hand tighter.

'Today, I will show you the westernmost tip of Japan, Stanley-san, which is also the southernmost tip,' he said. 'There we will see many wonderful things, including the first cherry blossoms of the year. Perhaps we will chase the opening blossoms all the way to the north.' He smiled warmly.

Stanley felt much better than he had the night before. He felt proud again to be Oda Nobu's personal ninja. Then something occurred to him. 'Oda-san,' he said. 'Where are your bodyguards today?'

Oda Nobu laughed. 'I'm afraid I gave them the wrong instructions. They are waiting for me at the movie studio. But so what?' He smiled and spread his hands. 'I have my own personal ninja with me. Why do I need bodyguards?'

That made Stanley feel proud, but also a little nervous. What if something happened? He was responsible for the great movie star's safety now. He and he alone. Then again, Oda Nobu was the most famous warrior on the planet. Who would dare try to hurt him?

Stanley thought about these things as

they settled into the comfortable chairs on the bullet train. Almost immediately, the train slid out of the station. Within moments, they were racing through the Japanese countryside.

'The *Shinkansen* travels at nearly three hundred kilometres per hour,' Oda Nobu said, as the towns and fields outside became a blur.

'Wow!' said Stanley. 'That's . . . that's nearly two hundred miles per hour!' He suddenly realised his teachers were right. Maths was really useful!

As they rode, Oda Nobu reached into his pocket and pulled out a small square of shiny paper. He made a few quick folds and twists, and there was a perfect

little frog!
He gave it
to Stanley,
pulled another
square of paper
from his pocket
and – *swish, snap,
snick!* – presented
Stanley with an elegant
long-necked crane.

'You're really good at origami,
Oda-san!' Stanley said. 'Almost as good as
you are at karate!'

Just then, the door of the train car
opened and a man walked in. He was
wearing a dark suit and dark glasses. He
noticed Oda Nobu and slowed down,

before walking past.

Stanley saw that Oda Nobu was suddenly frowning and tightly gripping the armrest of his seat.

'Oda-san!' Stanley said. 'Are you all right?'

Oda Nobu released his grip on the armrest. He nodded. 'Stanley-san,' he said, 'I must tell you something.'

For a few moments, Oda Nobu stared out the window at the hills rushing by. 'You and I are very much alike, Stanley-san,' he said at last. 'When I look at you, I see myself as a young boy.'

Stanley was stunned. 'You were flat, too?'

Oda Nobu laughed. 'No. But I was also

different. In my own way.' He turned to face Stanley. 'Look at me, Stanley-san. What do you see?'

Stanley smiled. 'I see the greatest movie star in the whole world!'

'Look more closely,' Oda Nobu said. 'What do you see when you watch my movies? You see this handsome face. This perfect smile. You hear this deep voice.

'Stanley-san, when I was your age, I wanted to be a karate master. But this face, and this smile and this voice made me different in other ways. And so, instead, I became an actor.'

Stanley listened quietly as Oda Nobu spoke.

'Instead of learning karate, I learned to

act,' he continued. 'I only *pretend* to know karate in the movies.'

'But I've seen your movies!' Stanley said. 'You are a master!'

Oda Nobu shook his head sadly. 'No, Stanley-san. When it is time for a big fight scene, I am not in it. It is my stunt double you see in the movies. He looks like me. But unlike me, he really is a karate master.'

Stanley couldn't believe what he was hearing.

'It is why I have bodyguards,' Oda Nobu said. 'On the movie screen, I can defeat all enemies. In the real world, I can defeat no one. I cannot even use my ninja star. It is only to make me appear tough.'

They rode in silence for a few minutes.

'Stanley-san,' Oda Nobu spoke. 'Here is a lesson I learned and that I wish to share with you. These things that make me special – this face, this smile, this voice – these things make me *what* I am, but not *who* I am. Do you understand?'

'I think so,' Stanley said. But he wasn't sure.

'*Who* I am is the boy who wanted to be a karate master,' Oda Nobu said, and he placed his hand over his heart. 'He is still in here. But I forgot about him for too long. I got confused by *what* I am. And now I think it is too late for him.'

Oda Nobu looked very serious now. 'Stanley-san, your flatness is what makes you special. But you must remember this:

being flat is *what* you are. It is not *who* you are. *Who* you are is a very bright, very funny, very curious young boy. It is who you are, flat or round. Always remember that, Stanley-san. Flat or round.'

Chapter Six

Surprise Visitors!

Oda Nobu had said that they would see many wonderful sights at the end of their journey. Stanley was not disappointed.

Everywhere he looked, he saw hundreds of cherry trees, each covered with thousands of pink blossoms. The blossoms swayed in a warm breeze blowing in from the East China Sea. Standing there in the

bright sunlight, under a deep-blue sky, Stanley thought it was the most beautiful sight he'd ever seen.

'Some day, Stanley-san,' Oda Nobu said, 'I will visit you in America. We will go together to your nation's capital, Washington, District of Columbia. Did you know that you have your own cherry trees there?'

Stanley said he hadn't known that.

'Oh, yes,' Oda Nobu said. 'In 1912, the people of Japan, as a sign of friendship, gave your country three thousand cherry trees. And now every spring, you have your very own Cherry Blossom Festival. Yes, I believe that some day we will go to it together.'

Oda Nobu smiled down warmly. But then he looked at Stanley more closely. He frowned. 'Stanley-san, I am sorry to say that you are still a little creased from being folded up last night. But I know something that may help.'

He hailed a taxi, and they took a short ride into the countryside. Looking out the window, Stanley saw something amazing: there in the distance was a volcano! Smoke rose in a dark plume from the crater at the top.

'Oda-san! Is that a real volcano?'

'Oh, yes,' Oda Nobu replied. 'Japan is a group of islands formed long ago by volcanoes. In fact, although Japan is a very small country, more than ten per cent of all the active volcanoes in the world are found here.'

The taxi pulled to a stop in front of a beautiful low building. Stanley recognised the words *inn* and *spa* among the Japanese characters on the sign.

'Here we are,' Oda Nobu said. 'Now you will discover one of the advantages of living in the land of volcanoes.'

They walked along a raked gravel path until they came to what looked like a gigantic stone swimming pool. The big volcano smoked in the distance, and the swimming pool appeared to be smoking, too.

'Throughout Japan you will find hot springs,' Oda Nobu said. 'The water comes from deep underground. It is heated by the same forces that make the volcano erupt.'

Stanley stood in the warm steam rising from the hot springs. He felt his wrinkles melting away. It felt so good.

Afterwards, he and Oda Nobu found a stone bench in a bonsai garden. They sat in silence, as Oda Nobu made one origami figure after another. When he finished one, he would hand it to Stanley.

Stanley lined the creatures along the bench. A dog. A cat. A grasshopper. A swan.

And then a small flat boy. Stanley knew who that was supposed to be.

'You have a brother, yes?' Oda Nobu

asked. Stanley nodded, and Oda Nobu made another paper boy, this one not so flat.

'And a mother and a father?' Oda Nobu said, and handed him a paper mother and father. Stanley sighed as he lined them up on the bench.

'You miss your family, don't you, Stanley-san?' Oda Nobu asked.

Stanley admitted that he did, very much.

'Well, I am sure they miss you, too, very much,' Oda Nobu said. 'Perhaps, then, it is time you went home.'

Thinking about how much he missed his family, Stanley could almost hear his mother's voice calling his name: *'Stanley Lambchop!'* The voice sounded so real!

'Stanley Lambchop, you were supposed to be down for breakfast four days ago!'

Stanley whirled around and there they were! His mother and his father and Arthur, all hurrying towards him.

Arthur was the first to reach him. 'Sorry,' he said. 'They made me tell where –' Arthur gasped as he recognised the man on the bench beside his brother. 'Oh, my gosh! It's the Seventeenth Samurai!' he cried, bowing several times. 'I salute you, Master Oda Nobu, greatest of all samurai warriors!'

Oda Nobu smiled and bowed to Arthur.

Mr and Mrs Lambchop joined them then. 'Young man,' Mr Lambchop said to Stanley sternly. '*Can* and *may* are two entirely different words. Just because you *can* mail yourself halfway around the world does not mean that you *may*. Your mother and I have been worried sick.'

'Sorry, Mum. Sorry, Dad,' Stanley said. He gave them big hugs and then hugged his brother, too. He was so happy to see them all! 'But I've been having such a good time! I ate raw fish, and I went to the movie studio, and do you know that Japan has more than ten per cent of the –'

'I don't want to interrupt you, dear,' Mrs Lambchop interrupted him. 'But I think we should get going. We shall hear all about your adventure on the way.'

Before anyone could say another word, the sky darkened. Stanley looked up, expecting to see heavy clouds blotting out the sun.

Instead he saw two ninjas, their faces hidden by black masks, racing along the rooftops on opposite sides of the garden.

Between them they held an enormous black cloth. At the far end of the garden, two more ninjas held the other corners of the cloth.

When the racing ninjas reached the end of the roof, they stopped. Then all four snapped the cloth and it billowed up like a huge parachute. Screaming 'Aiiii-*eeeeee*!'

in unison, they leaped high in the air and floated down into the garden.

The next second, Stanley was struggling to untangle himself from the black cloth that now covered him and his family and Oda Nobu. All of them were shouting in panic.

Then, loudest of all, Stanley heard Oda Nobu call, 'Stanley-san!

You must help me! I am being kidnapped!'

The Lambchops struggled for another long minute before Stanley was finally able to find the edge of the cloth. He quickly pulled it from the others and, looking around in the bright sunshine, his heart nearly stopped.

Oda Nobu was gone.

Chapter Seven

Kidnapped!

'Oda Nobu's been kidnapped!' cried Arthur. 'What should we do?'

'Seems to me it's those ninjas who should be worried,' chuckled Mrs Lambchop. 'If your famous friend is half the fierce warrior you boys say he is, I believe they'll have their hands full!'

'Still, Harriet, a crime has been committed,' Mr Lambchop reminded his wife. 'We must call the police at once and give them our report.'

Stanley shook his head. 'Oda Nobu made me his personal ninja,' he said. 'It was my responsibility to protect him, and I didn't. Now it is my responsibility to find him.'

George Lambchop put a hand on his older son's shoulder. 'Your mother and I have always taught you boys to live up to your responsibilities. However, there's school on Monday. That's a responsibility, too.'

'And besides,' Arthur said, 'all Oda Nobu has to do is use his Incredible Kick of

Catastrophe. Those ninjas will wish they'd never been born!'

Stanley thought sadly about what Oda Nobu had confided in him. The movie star was probably very afraid right now. And if the kidnappers found out he couldn't protect himself, his career would be over. 'No,' he told his family. 'I must save him.'

'But where are we going to start?' asked Arthur.

Stanley looked all around the garden. Something on the ground near the gate caught his attention. He walked over and picked it up.

'How about here?' he said, and held it up for the others to see.

It was an origami star, made from Oda Nobu's shiny paper.

Stanley's family followed him, as he looked for more paper stars. 'There!' Stanley called time after time as he ran ahead to pick up another one. 'This way!'

They hurried along like this for hours. Mrs Lambchop, who was in excellent shape because of daily exercise, greatly enjoyed the hike. But Mr Lambchop found himself huffing and puffing. 'Too much time behind the desk at the office,' he said. 'I guess this should be a good lesson for me.'

Eventually, the stars led them to a footbridge that crossed a stream and then ran along a long row of trees. Finally, just as the sun was about to set, they came to a lake.

At the shore, Stanley found one more paper star. He pointed to an island in the middle of the lake. On the island was a beautiful little pagoda. 'There,' Stanley said. 'That's where Oda Nobu is.'

'But how are we going to get there?' Arthur asked. 'I don't see any boats.'

Stanley thought a little and then smiled.

'Who wants to go first?' he asked. Then he lay down and slipped on to the lake's surface.

One by one, Stanley ferried his family across to the island. He kicked as quietly as he could. In a few moments, they were all together again, crouching in the darkness outside the pagoda.

'Now what?' asked Arthur.

'Lift me up, Arthur,' Stanley said. 'I want to look in this window.'

Arthur gave his brother a boost, and Stanley peeked in the window. He did not see the four ninjas, but he did see Oda Nobu, gagged and tied to a chair, with his wrists bound together in his lap.

Stanley hopped down. 'He's in there,'

he reported. 'They have him tied up.'

'So what should we do?' asked Arthur.

Stanley tried to think like a ninja. He remembered what Oda Nobu had said about the art of stealth. He looked down at the last origami star in his hand.

'I have a plan, Arthur,' he said. 'Fold me up exactly as I say. First, my left foot to my right shoulder. Next . . .'

The Ninja Star

Arthur crept quietly up the steps of the pagoda. He held an origami star next to his ear. But this wasn't one of Oda Nobu's paper stars.

This star was his brother, Stanley Lambchop.

'OK, Arthur, this is it,' Stanley said. His voice was muffled, folded up as he was.

'When we get to the door, knock loudly. When the door opens, throw me in as hard as you can. Straight at Oda Nobu. And then run! If they come after you, you and Mum and Dad have to swim for the shore.'

'Gee, Stanley, I don't think I like this plan.'

'We have to be as brave and daring as ninjas now,' Stanley told his brother. 'Oda Nobu is counting on us.'

Arthur took a deep breath. He raised the Stanley-star up, ready to throw, and knocked. In a moment, the door opened, and there stood . . .

Four smiling girls!

Stanley stared from under his ankle.

'Um, wait a minute, Arthur,' he began.

Too late. Arthur, now thinking like a ninja, threw Stanley as hard as he could. Oda Nobu's eyes widened as he watched the ninja star fly right for his head!

Stanley flew straight and true, the way a ninja star should. He hit Oda Nobu on the forehead and then bounced to the floor.

'Oda-san, it's me, Stanley!' he shouted. If Oda Nobu hadn't been tied down, he would have shot off the chair with shock.

Stanley tried with all his might to get to Oda Nobu's hand. On the second try,

Oda Nobu reached him, and snapped his fingers – and Stanley unfurled.

Stanley pulled the tape from Oda Nobu's mouth and then began to untie him.

'*Arigato*, Stanley-san! Thank you!' Oda Nobu whispered, as he rubbed his wrists. 'Those are the craziest fans ever!'

'Those girls?' Stanley asked. '*Those girls* are the ones who kidnapped you?'

Oda Nobu shuddered. 'The craziest!' he repeated.

'Are they dangerous?' Stanley asked.

Oda Nobu stuck his head around the corner to see into the other room. He broke into a big smile. 'Perhaps you should ask your brother,' he suggested.

Stanley looked into the other room. There was Arthur, beaming with happiness. He was surrounded by the four girls, who were folding little origami animals and giving them to him.

Oda Nobu and Stanley marched straight up to Arthur and the girls. Oda Nobu said something to the girls in Japanese. His words were harsh, and the girls looked frightened.

Stanley couldn't understand what Oda Nobu was telling them, but then at the end he heard, 'Flat Stanley!' At this, the girls turned to look at him,

wide-eyed with their hands to their mouths.

Then all of a sudden they were around him, laughing and taking pictures.

'Hey!' Arthur said. 'Mariko! Cho! Taki!

Hana! What about me?'

But the girls had forgotten all about Arthur. And, it seemed, Oda Nobu.

But Oda Nobu had not forgotten about them. He spoke sternly again, and all four girls hung their heads as they listened.

Mr and Mrs Lambchop appeared at the pagoda's front door.

'We will now return to the inn,' Oda Nobu told them. 'I will telephone the parents of these very disrespectful girls.'

At the inn, Arthur and Stanley watched as four taxis pulled away. In each was one very sorry girl and two very angry parents.

Then Oda Nobu's limousine pulled up.

Oda Nobu bowed to Mr and Mrs Lambchop. 'Your sons have performed as the most honourable, the most fearless of ninjas this evening. I insist you accompany me to Tokyo where you will stay as my guests as long as you wish.'

Tokyo

The next morning, everyone got up very early. 'I'm afraid we must leave on this evening's plane, as the boys have school on Monday,' Mrs Lambchop told Oda Nobu. 'But it would be lovely to spend the day sightseeing.'

'Very well,' said Oda Nobu. 'You must allow me to be your personal tour guide

of Tokyo, at your service.'

In that one day, he took the Lambchops everywhere.

On a private tour of the Imperial Palace.

To an aquarium, where they stood in a glass tunnel to watch electric eels and piranhas and sea horses challenge each other above them.

To the zoo, where they saw giant pandas and king penguins.

To a sumo match, where Stanley saw the roundest men he'd ever seen. Arthur couldn't help himself. 'Be careful, Stanley,' he joked. 'Those guys could flatten you!'

And then, of course, to the movie

studio, where Oda Nobu introduced the Lambchops all around.

At dusk, the limousine drew up in front of Oda Nobu's home again. Inside, the Lambchops were delighted to find four handsome kimonos waiting for them.

Stanley knew what this meant. He led his family down the hall to the tearoom, where Oda Nobu was already seated on

the straw mat. He sat down again as he had learned, and gestured for his family to follow his example. Oda Nobu bowed to him and passed him the bowl of tea. Stanley bowed to Oda Nobu and took a sip. Then Oda Nobu caught his eye and nodded to Mrs Lambchop. Stanley bowed to his mother and passed her the tea. Then he did the same for his father and his brother.

Oda Nobu gave Stanley a proud smile.

'Wow,' Arthur said, making a face after his sip of tea. 'This tastes kind of –'

'Interesting!' Stanley said quickly. 'I agree, Arthur!'

Mrs Lambchop gave Stanley a proud smile, too.

And then it was time to go to the airport. At the gate, as the Lambchops' flight was announced, Oda Nobu bowed deeply to Stanley.

'Stanley-san, you have given me a great gift,' he said. 'You have reminded me of *who* I am again. Not just *what* I am.'

Stanley smiled and shook Oda Nobu's hand. 'And you'll come with me to the

Cherry Blossom Festival next year? In Washington, D.C.?'

'Oh, yes, you may count on it. You will always be my personal ninja, and I will always be your most humble friend.'

The Lambchops waved goodbye to Oda Nobu and marched down the Jetway to their plane. As they boarded, the flight attendant took their tickets and looked puzzled. 'Only three tickets?' she asked. 'But there are four of you.'

'But only three of us need seats,' Mr Lambchop said. He sat down and then tucked Stanley neatly into the seat pocket in front of him.

Everyone had a hearty chuckle about the handiness of Stanley's shape before buckling up for the safe flight home.

'Mariko made this one!' Arthur pinned an origami owl to the bulletin board in his bedroom.

'And Cho made this one!' An origami turtle.

'And Taki!' A paper rabbit.

'And Hana!' Arthur tacked a paper . . . *something* to the bulletin board. 'What about you, Stanley? Did you bring home any souvenirs?'

Stanley sat on his bed, looking glumly at a photograph. 'Oh, I have this, I guess,' he said. It was a picture of Oda Nobu, looking fierce in his samurai robes, holding his hands menacingly above his head. *To Stanley, Fight strong, Oda Nobu* was written across the photo.

Stanley looked away. He felt sad for some reason.

'Stanley Lambchop!' Mr Lambchop called up the stairs. 'Express mail for Stanley Lambchop!'

Stanley jumped up and raced down the stairs. Moments later he returned, holding an envelope. The stamps in the corner were Japanese.

'Open it up!' Arthur cried.

Stanley did. He pulled out a photograph and a letter, which he then read aloud.

'Dear Stanley-san, here is the real me. I can never thank you enough for showing me who I am, rather than what I am. I will see you soon. And when I do, I promise I will be at least a green belt!'

Stanley looked at the photo. There was Oda Nobu, standing in a line of karate students. A white belt was knotted around his waist. He was smiling broadly.

Stanley could not have felt prouder. He tacked the photo to the bulletin board and then turned and bowed to Arthur.

'Prepare to fight, Arthur-san!' he cried. 'Prepare to be defeated!'

'Never!' Arthur said, as he leaped up, bounced high on his bed and landed with a *boom* on the opposite side of the room. 'It is you who will be defeated, Stanley-san!'

'Boys!' Mrs Lambchop called up the stairs. 'Arthur! Stanley! The bookshelves are wobbling!'

'Can we have a little quiet time?' pleaded Mr Lambchop from his study.

'Sorry, Mum! Sorry, Dad!' the boys called back in unison. And then they went right back to what they were doing.

Turn the page to read about Stanley's Big Mountain Adventure...

Chapter One

Ready, Set . . .

'Sleeping bags?' George Lambchop called out to his wife, Harriet.

'Check!' answered Mrs Lambchop. 'Wholesome snacks for the boys?'

'Check!' replied Mr Lambchop.

The Lambchop family was preparing for their vacation to Mount Rushmore in the Black Hills of South Dakota. They were each very excited about the adventure.

Mr Lambchop was excited because he was going to collect another state park sticker for the rear window of the car.

Mrs Lambchop was excited because she was going to learn more about the history of South Dakota.

Their younger son, Arthur, was excited because he was hoping to meet some real, live cowboys.

And Stanley, the Lambchops' older son, was excited because he was going somewhere nobody would recognise him.

Not long ago, Stanley had awakened to find that his enormous bulletin board had fallen upon him during the night. Since then, the family had gotten used to having a flattened boy in the house. But when he ventured outside, he often caused a commotion: 'Look, Marge! There he is . . . the famous flattened kid! Wonder what new adventure he's up to now?' Or, 'Say there, Flatty, mind if we take a picture?'

The truth is, both Lambchop brothers were getting a bit tired of all the attention Stanley was getting. It would be nice, they agreed, to get away someplace where people didn't make such a fuss.

'Well, I think we're ready,' said Mr Lambchop, surveying the mountain of suitcases and camping equipment in the hall.

'Not quite, dear,' replied Mrs Lambchop. 'Remember, we still have to consult

Doctor Dan about Stanley's travel needs. Better safe than sorry.'

'Well, the boy is still flat,' Doctor Dan pronounced, when he finished his examination.

'Yes, we know that,' said Stanley's father. 'We were wondering whether such a trip would be suitable for Stanley in his present condition. Mount Rushmore's elevation is 5,725 feet, for one thing. And we'll be travelling by automobile along the scenic highways at a fairly high velocity.'

Here Mrs Lambchop interrupted her husband with a chuckle. 'Not too high a velocity, of course,' she said.

Mr Lambchop smiled at his wife's joke. Both she and Mr Lambchop were always careful to obey local speed limits. 'Still,' he said, 'we did feel it would be wise to check with you.'

'It's a good thing you did. More people should be concerned about the effects of travel on the body. The human being is a very complex organism. Even we doctors, with our extensive knowledge, don't completely understand it.'

'Oh, dear,' Mrs Lambchop said anxiously. 'Will it be all right for Stanley to come with us?'

'Of course!' said Doctor Dan. 'I can't think of any reason why not!'